The Oracle and the Dreamer

New Earth Parables

by
Mary Saint-Marie/Sheoekah

The Oracle and the Dreamer

New Earth Parables

Published by Ancient Beauty Studio, www.marysaintmarie.com

ISBN: 978-0-9646572-3-6 (sc)

All artwork by Mary Saint-Marie

Front Cover Art: *Heart Essence*

Back Cover Art: *purity manifest*

Page 14 Art: *realm of purity*

Page 126 Art: *Being Here*

Credit for NASA Public Domain Image of M35: Atlas Image obtained as part of the Two Micron All Sky Survey (2MASS), a joint project of the University of Massachusetts and the Infrared Processing and Analysis Center/ California Institute of Technology, funded by the National Aeronautics and Space Administration and the National Science Foundation.

to the 10 Blue Kachinas
from the Realm of Purity
and
to Every One and Everything and Everyplace

Contents

Acknowledgments

I deeply acknowledge the One Essence that is arising as a new earth culture.

I deeply acknowledge the Indivisible…visible. The Undivided One.

I thank all the awakened souls holding space for the new earth. I thank you for inspiring others to awaken and to be living in harmony with each other and with the earth and with the sky.

I thank my daughters for helping me re-visit innocence and purity while they were young. What a gift!

I thank my muse friend, Laura Daen, for being "the first listener" to these parables and for sharing numinous feedback at the depth that I was aware of them.

I thank Aaron Rose for conscious and beautiful designing of the book and its cover.

I also thank him for being ever vigilant to the soul voice of the book, as it lands into form.

I thank Lewis Mitchell for his assistance with preparing the images for the book.

I thank the following ones for technical support:

Art image work by Light Source Creations, Lewis Mitchell, Medford, Oregon

Design and Layout by Aaron Rose, Mount Shasta, California

Photography by Rebecca Allen, Mount Shasta, California

Editing by Mary Saint-Marie and Aaron Rose

I thank all inner and outer ones who have assisted me to be the Emptiness to feel, then hear, the stories as they translated into words, cadence, and tone.

Introduction

These parables began to come to me on Thanksgiving of 2014, as I retreated in solitude in my home. They continued for the next 4 ½ months. Usually I did not know when one would come. And occasionally I would hear a couple words or a phrase during the day. This alerted me to the inner listening to the Presence.

The parables began to arrive in my consciousness entirely on their own. I did not call to stories nor did I pursue them. I just became very empty and open with inner listening and inner Awareness.

The parables began to float gently in from the subtle realms. I would lose the thread if I was distracted by the tiniest thought or external situation.

The stories, like my art and other writing, quietly and mysteriously invite one inward...into the Emptiness.

These stories have a great simplicity. They are as poetic odysseys into the realms of purity.

They may inspire a great longing for the Great Emptiness. They herald a new way.

The stories are universal. They give voice to the eternal. They are simple manifestations of the new earth, speaking and voicing with few words and almost no description.

The reader or listener is invited within to explore their own experience of "tonal vision" and "essence vision." For in the stories, the reader or listener must "see for themselves." Soul vision brings with it...exaltation.

These parables are living stories of being. They call us first into the universal archetypal realms and then beyond into the Realm of the Real, into Pure Consciousness. They call us each to "see" the new earth from our own unique perspective and to live that which we see within. Share it with the world.

As Lao Russell would say, "Give love a body."

The Parables

The Watcher:
A Girl from the Stars

The little girl sat there.
She sat there for three years.
She just sat there on a little stool.
She sat in the middle of the room.
She sat staring into space…or
perhaps it was into stars…
She sat smiling.
And she was silent.
Words were there none.

Her mother noticed. Others did not.
Her mother knew this was to be kept
secret, silent.
The social milieu frowns on such
seemingly asocial behavior.
Note the word seemingly.
It has a great story to tell.

The social agreement is to remove
such ones from the herd.
They are unique, different;
they don't fit the homogeneous mold.

The mother knew.
She knew the little girl was doing well
and she knew the little girl was happy.

The smile...it was there.
It was always there.
The smile...it spoke...

Even the mother would say...
it is time for a nap or time to go to bed.
The little girl would smile and go to sleep.
And the smile was there.

Four years of age arrived,
The little girl found nature.
The little girl found trees.
And birds and squirrels.
She found turtles and crabs and on...

High into the trees she climbed.
Embraced. Content. Joyful.
She still smiled.

The little girl found an escape.
She escaped the anger, the fights,
the alcoholic mom and dad.

The little girl witnessed both silence
and the world around her.
She watched.
She noticed what others were doing.

The little girl was a watcher.

The little girl watched.
She watched everything.
She noticed that she was different somehow.
She noticed that she was learning how to be
"in the world."
She found it strange.

The little girl found it challenging.
There were so many that were sad or angry.
The little girl could see through the masks.
She could see the call for help.

The little girl thus began her soul expression.
She was there for her mother, a sister...
and many friends.
The years came and went.

The little girl grew. Now she was "smiley"...
Many called her "smiley"...

The girl did not yet know of the out of balance
human beings upon this planet.
Creating wars everywhere.
At every level of society...from homes to nations...

The girl still thought her little family
was the only family with so much pain.
And so it is she learned.
The local family on out to global families,

imbalance does often reign.
And the girl noticed...they think this is normal.

Teenage and college years arrived
and it became very difficult to be unique.
The girl now worked to fit in, to be liked.
She entered a career that she did not want.
It was an acceptable field for a woman.

The smile began to fade. Like a flower in the fall...
it began to disappear...

So far life on planet earth was traumatic.
Joy seemed to come to people when they bought
or ate things or drank.
Joy seemed to come when entertainment was around.
Joy seeming to come when all were wildly dancing.

So it is...the watcher began to dance.
She wildly moved whenever the music came.
It seemed to clear the field,
like her first three years of sitting.
And the ensuing years high in the trees.

The watcher danced. Joy arose.
And still her life's expression was not right.
She had no sense of the direction to take.
Life delivered a near death experience,
a seeming disaster.

And now, the watcher watched within.

The watcher viewed her life, past, present, future...
simultaneously in the Now.
She watched it through the lens of Joy.
An exalted joy never known by the human being.

The watcher glimpsed "spiritual being"
in the second of the head-on car collision.
The watcher could now see light
around all living things.
The watcher had deepened into the experience
of being in the world, not of the world.

Slowly, the watcher saw humanity living
in the market place of beliefs.

Buying and selling beliefs.
And living the beliefs.

Living the beliefs like a vast tainted coating
covering transparency.

Slowly...the watcher saw more and more
of her own beliefs.

Slowly...the watcher learned to ignore them,
let them go.
They returned to the field of light
and her light grew brighter.

Slowly...the watcher allowed herself to identify
with the light of Consciousness.

And "slowly" began to be no more.
With spiritual identity came a hastening,
a quickening.

And in the watcher...the smile emerged.
She could feel where to cast...to ones in need...

The watcher deepened in soul expression.
The watcher began
to draw, paint, sculpt, write, sound…
and thus began the flow…
The watcher did see the flow…
as the sacred river of life…
The watcher did notice
that the flow caused joy to arise…
The watcher did notice
she was now living from the inside out.
She did notice that more and more
she could ignore outer pressures.
The only "press" remaining was Soul Expression.

And, so it is, that the watcher watched inwardly.
Learning that we may express outwardly.

And, so it is,
that the watcher watched and waited for others,
so ready to be in that illumined flow
of the river of life…the river of convergence…
so prepared by Life to nod yes!

And the watcher noticed Life had a simplicity,
though the world shouted complex, difficult.

The watcher knew. And she knows.
The watcher knows humanity knows.
Prior to mind...they know...
The watcher knows there is only Consciousness...
And, beyond that, the watcher disappears...
and arises...pure I Am Awareness...

The watcher smiles.

November 26, 2014, Thanksgiving Day
Lake Shastina, California

The Worshippers:
And the Sound of Star Light
And this One from the Stars

It was 2015
and most of the world
had become worshippers.
The people...they worshipped money.
They worshipped clothes. And cars and jewelry.
They worshipped houses. They worshipped status.
They worshipped the intellect
and the ensuing technology.

O how they worshipped the external world
and its promise of safe, secure and stable.
O how they worshipped the external world
and its promise of happiness.
Even food...it was worshipped...
as a source of happiness.

And with all this fullness of life,
a great emptiness fell upon the masses.
And the people...they worked even harder...
and struggled even...to fill the emptiness.
The chant became...more, more, more.

The quality of the more no longer mattered.
It could be replaced.
There was more.
Always...there was more.
Quantity was worshipped feverishly.

No longer were there filters
that identified quality or purity.
Quantity became a god.
Pollution was the fallout.

Pollution and the more and more
became the nemesis of the worshippers.
The worshipping of quantity
blinded the worshippers.
They could only see more, more, more.

And arrived unto these lands
from a far away star was a One.
This One sang a sound.
This sound of star light entered unto the world.
Eyes began to open. And ears.
And hearts...everywhere.

The people stood mystified. They felt a something.
What did they feel, they did ask.
They asked themselves.
They began to ask each other.

They stopped what they were doing.
There was a current.
It was barely perceptible.
An awareness...
birthed of this force.
A silent call did await within their hearts.
The road to the altar of more no longer satisfied.

Yet the people saw no other road.
They stood.

They were silent.
They had eyes to see. They gazed about them.
Past concrete and cars and commerce everywhere,
they saw a flower.
It seemed different.
They looked. They smelled.
Its essence did enter upon their brain
and seemed to have a voice.

At first, they were fearful
to tell their neighbors or friends.
They were even afraid to tell their family.
People would laugh at them. And ridicule.
And speak behind their backs.

At first, they were cautious.
They wanted to belong.
They had not yet realized
that in the recognition of the flower's voice of scent
that they had found belonging.
They belonged to Nature.
To the All.

A few brave people told each other.
They shared their secret world.
And the numbers grew.
People at first only whispered of the flower.
As others spoke aloud of this, news of a new way,
that was not a road or even a path, was upon them.
They began to gather.

At first they gathered around this simple flower.
Never had a scent so affected them.
They sat silent in the unknowing.
They inhaled the essence.
They listened.

The One from a far away star did notice.
These people had smelled the essence from the stars,
carried by the flower.

And still the people sat.
The worshipping of more had stopped.
They felt different.
They liked what they felt.

The people began to share this new feeling.
The news began to spread.
No longer were the ads for more watched.
The tvs sat silent in the homes.

It was strange.
More little white flowers began to appear.
More people gathered.
They would sometimes speak of miracles.
The people who had been there,
from the beginning of the flower's appearance,
quieted them.
They asked them to feel the peace
that descended unto the world
through these tiny flowers.

A peace began to over light the growing group
that gathered where these flowers did appear.
They had never felt such peace.
It seemed to be that peace
beyond the understanding of their minds.
They dropped conjecture.

A peace did fill the scented air.
And it did fill their hearts.
This was a peace that had no name.
It had only been prayed for,
through the eons of war and battle.

The battle and its cry did cease to be.
No people listened to its call.
Its life...it was no more.

The One from a far away star was not seen.
She saw that the scent of star light
was permeating every heart.

Some people who heard of this gathering feared.
They feared these people were under a spell.
At first, they stayed away.
Far away.

And more flowers did appear.
The scent of peace filled the air.
Gently...wind did spread it.
It was moved around the earth.

Eyes opened. And ears. And hearts everywhere.

People began to give.
They gave everything they could.
They gave their gifts.
Some gave food; others...clothes.
The giving grew.
And regiving was upon them.
With no trying, they were showered with abundance.

And now appeared a filter.
A filter, a lens for purity.
Pollution was shunned.
No need to ban, for pure hearts had the filter.
This filter of purity was found to be inherent.
It just had not been noticed.

This new way of giving spread across the lands.
People marveled.
They rejoiced in simple giving.
Life long desires were fulfilled.
It appeared to be magic, but they knew.

With eyes open and ears and hearts,
the people began to see all of nature.
They saw nature as the source of the gifts
they were giving.

With this new found giving, the peace grew.
It filled all spaces.
It filled everywhere.

The people turned from the road
of the worshipping of more.
The road lay desolate behind them.
And children began to plant
flowers along the road.

Purity was in every heart.
Purity was understood by the heart.
And the hearts everywhere began to beat as One.

The people felt the One.

This One did sing a sound of star light.
And there were ears to hear.

A new earth did appear before them.
And awe walked across earth's stage.
Everywhere, in everyone, was awe.

People looked around them.
And they did see.
They had eyes to see.

Everything did glow.
The light from everywhere and everything
was upon this One.

The One joined hands and hearts.

The flowers were made of light.
They radiated.

And the One did know.
The Timeless Realm was upon them.
No one looked back upon the stage of time.
Stars were seen in eyes of everyone.

And this One did sing a sound of star light.
The sound did fill the earth.

Reminders of ages past did disappear.
Traces of time could be found nowhere.
Thinking was not needed,
as Awareness did behold.

Quickly...
beholding became the norm.
Silence filled the air.
Even followed by deeper silence.

Words...there were none.

And this One did sing a sound of star light.

Behold...a new earth...

January 22–23, 2015
Lake Shastina, California

When I sat down to write on the 22nd, I immediately felt like I was breaking the habit of believing that I can write best when driving or in the night or in pre-dawn or dawn hours. Or painting. I can be empty and receive anytime... the words from the infinite.

My friend, the first listener, said, "These stories are Passages of Purity."

an om rang out

An om rang out.
The men began it.
Others joined in.
A processional began.

Where were they going...the others wondered.
It was dusty.
The darkness approached.

Silence was everywhere, except for the om.

After some time on the dusty road,
they began to hear It.
What was It?
Sounds began to be heard between the oms.
Such beauty began to pour in.
Looks of enchantment arose on faces.

Some wept softly.
Others turned their heads.

They looked everywhere.
Nothing was there to be seen.

And It grew louder.
It seemed to the others to be magic.
And yet…no magicians arrived.

The oms continued.
Soft, low and drone-like.
The stillness stood undisturbed
by both the oms and the It that caused ones to weep.

There were no tears of sadness.
Yet…there were tears of the quietest joy.
It was filling hearts.

No one tried to understand.
An innocence seemed to over-light
and enter into them.
Each time they heard It, they did open.

The oms served as a portal to It.

And now, heads rose to the sky.
The sounds of It filled the sky.
It was everywhere.

Some did open their mouths and It poured forth.
Gentle, almost imperceptible.

The sky now was dark.
Yet It seemed to illumine all space with sound.

And others began to sound.

It was in the sky.
It was in their hearts.
It was everywhere.

Not a one asked…how could this be?
They no longer cared.

Many had heard rumors of a new earth.
For eons even.
Stories were told.

Myths were promulgated.
Movies seen of other worlds.

This...was very different.
These others were the Living story now.
No questions arose.
Or resistance.
Nor even desire.
A great calm was upon them.

Disruption...there was none.

They arrived in a great open space.
A circle formed.
Luminous sound was heard.
And some could see.
They could behold.
They could behold this realm.

Silently....they all said yes.

They said yes to a world prior to fear.

Prior to fear and hate and rage.
Prior to battles.
And opposition.

Life prior to the oms was forgotten.
Quickly forgotten.
It was as if it never were.

A gentle wind arose.
It seemed to blow the past away.
An unremembered oblivion.
There were no waves goodbye.
No words.
The past just disappeared.

They were all Here!

And they knew.
They knew that the past, present and future
were here now.
One.

And they noticed.
They noticed that beliefs did not exist.
They noticed all sickness had fallen away.

An era...just gone.

The three men continued to om.
The others sat.
Dawn arrived.
Never was a word spoken.

Words were no more.
It did seem magic.
Yet it was simple, natural...
as if It had always been.

The others stood.
Silently they returned to the village.
All was the same.
Yet nothing looked the same.
There was a soft glow.

Movements and changes were a liquid flow.
The Dance of the One was felt by everyone.
A sense of separation ceased to be.

The Timeless One...here and now...

Awe filled the village.

In the distance...an om rang out...

February 10, 2015, 8–10 p.m.
Lake Shastina, California

I was sitting quietly in the evening reflecting and contemplating the word dedication. I became aware of dedication as an opening. Dedication opens inner portals. Some call it grace. It is the heaven world. The heaven world...lived.

And then just sitting quietly, while listening to an om cd, I heard ever so subtly the words...an om rang out. I wrote them down. The story ensued slowly and sweetly...with its magic of the It filling me.

A friend, the first listener, was reminded of the three wise men. It is certain that "It" is the Christed divine energies of the purest love. And it is available now.

The Oracle and the Dreamer

Few had seen the oracle.
Many winters had come and gone.
No one had counted the years.
They were many.

The ones who saw the oracle
said her eyes shone like the stars.
They saw her walking in the woods
when the sun was low.
When day kissed the night, she appeared.

She gazed everywhere.
Nature seemed to love her gaze.
The leaves, the flowers,
even ants seemed to gaze upon her.
Something flowed between them
and they embraced.

The few who saw said it was another world.

Some were even frightened,
as though she was a witch of stories past.
But some said they saw flickers of strange lights.
These were drawn closer.
They even thought they felt something
inside of them.

One day the wind was blowing.
It was a darkened day.
One watched a child walk into the forest.
The child looked only straight ahead.
The entire forest seemed to greet the child.
Animals had no fear of this child being.
They ate and played as if the child belonged.

The one who watched continued on.
He was not curious.
He seemed unable to stop his steps.

The child was unaware of this one.

The child walked on, as if a path was there.

No path could be seen.

It seemed as if time stood still.
Or disappeared even.

All clocks were far away.
It seemed a distant past.

Indeed, all outside the forest home
seemed a distant past.

The child stopped.
She looked about.
Her eyes began to glow.
This light flowed like a river.
It reached the oracle.

The oracle sat in stillness beneath a great tree.
The branches reached out creating a great space.
It was a space to meet.

And like the branches, the oracle reached out.

The child was welcomed such.
The child curled within the branch-like arms
and fell asleep.

In these arms, the child did dream.
She dreamed beyond clocks and even cars.
She dreamed beyond two powers.
She dreamed of home.
Humanity's home.

The home...it had no place.
No location.
It could not be found on a map.

The home...it had to be dreamed.
And so...the child did dream.
She had come to dream.
Without the dream, all would perish.

The one who watched knew nothing of dreams.
He knew nothing of perishing.
He seemed to be motionless in this field of light.

A simple witness.

That it was all so strange escaped him.
An unfamiliar feeling rested upon him.
He was content.
Even his mind sat silent.

The dream continued.
The dream contained the answers.
A world beyond want was seen.
And known.

O how the child did dream.

O how the flowers sang out.
And the stars.
Even the stones.

The child did see. The child did dream.

Each day this child entered upon this forest floor.
And she dreamed.

Each day this dream entered the field.

Weeks passed and months.
People everywhere
felt the unfamiliar feeling rest upon them.
They were content.

Clocks were unplugged.
Cars sat empty.
People began to stream into the forest.
Silently they streamed.

The people could feel the dream.
They could feel the dream awaken.

They, the people, were the awakening dream.

The girl awoke.
Innocence radiated everywhere.
And purity.

And, still, few had seen the oracle.

I was driving home to Lake Shastina. Out of the silence, I heard the words, The Oracle. It was very clear that another modern parable was coming.

54

she sings to the earth

She sings to the earth.
Sweetly...she does sing unto the earth.
The earth does listen.
Ears are everywhere.

A sweetness fills the very air.
It cannot be seen.
It is felt.
It is felt by everything.

Every single thing does stop.
A great reverence
falls over the land.
And even across the sea.

Every thing does hear the song.
Miles no longer matter.
There is a great hush.

The song...it falls upon everything.

Arms raise and hands.
Even faces.
As if to take in the song.

Underneath the song...is silence.

Everywhere hearts open.
Hearts long closed...do open.
Hearts long hiding...open wide.

And still...she sings.

Fear has fallen away. It exists no more.
Not a trace.
A memory...disappeared.

Even the animals.
Free of fear.
And free in this pervading song.

An era...borne inside a song.
O the song...it touches everyone.

It touches everything.
And even everywhere.

Wonder begins to grow.

The Unspeakable...now speaks.
Through song...it does speak.

Wonder is everywhere.
No place is left untouched.

And it...is seen.
It is seen that it has always been. Always.
And even ever lasting.

It used to be called enchantment.
Mere fantasy.
No more.
It has always beckoned.
It beckoned from no where.
It was always here.
It was always here...inside the song.

And still…she sings.

No one knew how she found the song.
Or even where.
No one even questions.

An era passing. Just gone.
No finale. Or fanfare.
No logos of remembrance.
Or endless chat of times past.

Era of wonder. Rapture even.
Thoughts…they are not needed.
A relic of the past.

Awareness rains upon them.
It rains upon the earth.
Awareness rains in every heart.

Ears listen. Eyes…they watch.
Hearts do sing.
Hearts everywhere sing to the earth.

Everything is singing.
Wonder has a voice.

And still…she sings.

There is no one to whisper to.
Or teach.
For everything has heard the song.
There is no dim past.
There is no past at all.

Questions don't arise.
Only joy.

Feet bare, she walks upon the earth.

And still…she sings.

February 16, 2015, 8:30 p.m.
Lake Shastina, California

My friend, the listener, said, "These stories are haunting and I can feel them beckoning from the depths."

tell the others this…

O…it cannot snow…they did say.
The climate was changing.
Everybody saw.
Now it was warm.
The mountain stood uncovered.
People talked.
Worry filled the air.

An old man sat nearby.
A very old man.
He had seen many winters.
Some had snow. Some did not.
He was calm. He did not talk.
Worry could not find his face.
It traveled elsewhere.
And no one noticed.

At times there arose a flurry of town talk.
Questions flew everywhere.
Answers…imagined.

And still...the snow was gone.

At times fear pierced the air.
Children cried.
No one knew why.
They could not see the fear.
The fear sometimes lingered.
It made dogs bark.
No one knew why.

One day someone noticed the very old man.
This one drew near.
The air felt different here.
How could that be?
Perhaps this one imagined it.
Understanding escaped. It seemed a mystery.
This one did stand upon a brink.
Two worlds...side by side.

This one...stepped even closer to the very old man.
It was certain. Yes...it was certain now.
Something strange was here.

It was unexpected.
It was invisible.

What can I say to others…this one did wonder.
They might not notice. Or even feel.
I might be alone.
Others may laugh.
They will joke…about me.

I can say nothing…this one did think.

O this one did not depart.
Closer to the very old man…this one did move.

The very old man felt his guest.
His eyes did open.
There had been no sleep.
Just a simple deepened rest.

The guest was startled.
Did he disturb this very old man?
Did the strange calm originate here?

The guest did gasp.
Words almost imperceptible began to come.
The very old man began to speak.
It was so quiet.
The guest drew closer.
Was he speaking to me...the guest did wonder.
The guest was silent.

Climate is consciousness.
This...the very old man did speak.
Draw near...he did speak.
You are playing a game. It is a serious game.
There are consequences. I say...do not play.

Tell others.

Tell others there is another way.
Tell others that way has always been.
It shall continue to be...even.
O how gullible they did become.
Believing that the game was real.
Believing in the fear.

Tell the others this.

Tell them of another Consciousness.
Tell them to look for no savior.
Tell them to leave herd consciousness.
Tell them to leave.

Tell them to leave this game that leads them.
Confusion covers them. Crying comes.

Tell the others this.

Tell them to sit.
Tell them to listen.
Tell them of this greater Consciousness.
Tell them to connect with this.
Their minds and hearts shall seem as One.

Tell them now.

The time is late.
But not too late.
The very old man repeated…it is not too late.

The very old man...he closed his eyes.
He was calm. He fell silent.

The guest was in a reverie.
His wondering was now...wonderment.
How did such a change come upon him?
He only heard the simple words.

The words did fall upon his heart.
The words embraced.
The words planted a new life within him.

The guest stood speechless.
Though he had been asked to speak.

The very old man repeated...tell the others this.

The guest did look about.
How did he miss the changes?
Others were drawing near. Many others.

O how is it he could see the world?

The entire world was seen.
And they gathered.
They began to gather.

They gathered everywhere.

And the guest began to speak.

To tell the others this.

February 17, 2015, 8:40–10:25 p.m.
Lake Shastina, California

and still…she came…

And still…she came.
No matter the anger.
Still…she came.
No matter the looks.
The stares.
Still…she came.

Dressed in love…she arrived.
Adorned…
in stillness.
The world stood still.

Silent…she walked among the trees.
Flowers everywhere felt her pass.
The sand upon the beaches felt her feet.

She stood tall.

She could hear Unheard sounds.
She could see the Unseen.

Why had she come? Why had she traveled here?
A planet of tears. And wars.
A planet where the stars were forgotten.

And still...she came.

She came...bringing memory.

She came...bringing memory...of a vastness.

Awareness of a vast emptiness.

An emptiness of great accord...
borne in consciousness.

An emptiness that holds everything.

And...yes...still...she came...

She was filled with stars and moons. And suns.
She told no one.
She could see.

They did not want to know.
And it mattered not.

The sun had sent her...
into this night of consciousness.
The sun had spoken...
With no words...the sun had spoken...
With no words...the sun announced the journey.

And...she came.

A time outside of time was coming.

She must be Here.

And there were others. Many others.
They...too...had come.

They...too...felt it.
They knew The Great Time was upon them.
It was upon them all.

Together...they had come to be Here.

Careers were not needed. Or fame.

They were heralds. And no one knew.

And starry nights mirrored their Vastness.

No longer could they hide away their Knowing.

No longer could they pretend.

Lightness filled the very air.

And no longer did they stare.

Awe was on tongues everywhere.

And prayers...stood in every heart.

Timelessness arose.
It spoke to no one.
It had no need.
It filled the Vastness.

Stars shone everywhere.

Everyone was Here...

Now...everyone was Here...

March 2, 2015, 9:40–11:25 p.m.
Mount Shasta, California

Upon hearing this story, my friend, the first listener, said, "Wow, I want to weep...beyond words...and yet...again the simple words say it all...it so brings eternity and the infinite worlds into the now."

O we all are oracles

O we all are oracles...the young boy says...

We all can see beyond the veils...
and hear and know...

We all can see beyond the veils...
for they shall disappear...

Underneath our thoughts, thinking and beliefs
is now...another world...

It sings...
It sings of happiness...the young boy says...
There is happiness...
alone...

The young boy throws up his arms...
in joy...
He begins to run...
In a meadowed land...

The oracle is here...one did say...
Faces everywhere do tighten...
Fright speaks on every face...
Tension borne of time walks upon the stage...

Joy flees...
Fear settles most everywhere...

The young boy runs...
In a meadowed land...
Fear runs after him...
It finds him not...

The young boy is clothed in joy...
He hears its call...
He laughs...
He runs...

Veils begin to fall...
Always the veils begin to fall...
the young boy says...
In joy...the veils begin to fall...

I see that I am you…
And you are me…

I see that nature glows…
Everything…it glows…

The boy is mad…one did say…
All turn and flee…
Fear companions all…

Only dust is seen upon the road…
All have turned and fled…

The young boy stands speechless…
Joy now fills the air…
He spins…
He dances…
He sits with flowers…

The boy…he understands…
The boy…he awaits…
The boy…awaits their knowing…

One day their clocks shall stop...
the young boy says...

The timeless one shall leap into hearts...
It shall leap into hearts everywhere...
Joy shall arise...

Fear shall disappear...the young boy says...
Fear shall be no more...

No one shall flee...
They shall bury fright...
It shall enter history as fiction...

Fear shall be no more...

Joy shall take its rightful place...
the young boy says...
It shall govern every heart...
It shall smile from every face...

O we all are oracles...the young boy says...

And he begins to run...
In a meadowed land...

March 15, 2015, 8:20–9:30 p.m.
Mount Shasta, California

This story began over a week earlier and I became very busy with life and I was not able to receive the rest until I became very empty.

This Village

He was there.
He had always been there.
The people had seen the old man.
It seemed...forever.

Everybody liked the old man.
They waved.
He waved back.

There was something in his eyes.
No one spoke of it. But everybody knew.

When anyone felt bad, they walked by the old man.
They waved.
Their eyes did touch.
He waved back.

No words were spoken.
No words were ever spoken.
No words need be spoken.

He lived in a world apart from them.
In the glance, they were transported.

They were transported; they knew not where.
They did not care.

Their cares did disappear. Even their questions.
They hummed. They whistled. Some even sang.

Like a mystery unsolved, happiness did appear.

The entire village knew this happiness.

Word spread.
People began to come from everywhere.
They traveled to this place.
This village.

They travelled to this place
where happiness was free.

It was free. And it was freedom.

Long years of bondage melted.
Sadness said goodbye.

And one cloudy day, he was not there.
The old man…he was not there.

He was not sitting where he always sat.
He was not waving as he always waved.
He was not glancing as he had always done.

Quiet crept over and through the village.

They all knew.
They all knew one day he would not be there.

The spot was empty. This was the day.

They all knew.
They all knew he had only come for a while.

They all knew.
They knew his glance was another world.

Silently the village had said yes.
Silently the village opened its heart.

And word did spread.
And the people...they came.
They came from everywhere.

They heard stories.
They heard stories from this one and that.

Everybody's story was personal.
And charged.
The people could not tell what charged the stories.

Nothing was written.
Nothing was ever written.

The old man never spoke. Nor did he write.

The village continued on.
They told their stories.
They told their stories to those who came.

Sometimes they just waved.
And sometimes they just glanced.

Happiness...it spread.

March 26, 2015, 5:30–6:10 p.m.
Sisson Meadow in the sun
Mount Shasta, California

I had gone to the meadow to walk, sit in the sun, and be silent. Unexpectedly I wrote the words "parables of the new earth" on a paper. Shortly after, this parable did come.

The Signs were Everywhere

The signs were everywhere.

Everybody saw them.
No one could see them.
No one could really see them.
Or read.

Each sign did tell a story.
A great story.
Every sign told a story of change.

A great change.
A story of great change was upon them all.

It was in the news.
It was in photos.
It was in experiences...in lives...
Around the world...it was felt...

What is it...everyone did ask.

What is it that causes all the weather? The chaos?
What is it that causes such suffering?
What is the cause?

Every one looked about them.
They saw the signs.
Some feared.
Many profited.
Many did worry.
Others did nothing.

And one could see.
One could see.

The woman was quiet.
She did not speak.

Hidden from sight, yet fully seen,
the signs appeared everywhere.

The woman could see.
The woman weathered many births.

The woman did know.
She did know they were signs of a greater birth.

The woman was silent.
Words never formed.
Nor did they flow.

Ones saw their own imaginings.
Ones did see beliefs appear.

The woman did see.
The woman...she did see...
The woman did see from beyond the stars...
The signs did light the sky.
The signs did portend the new.

The signs were everywhere.

She did not ask...why don't they see.
She did not ask...

The woman did see.

She did see the heaven's script.
She did read.
She did know.

A great birth was upon them.
A great birth was upon them all.
Each tiny sign…a part of this birth…
Each tiny sign…singing of this birth…
And large signs…all did sound the note…

Many stories passed through lips.
Many fell away.
Many passed to others.

Separate stories lingered.
Stories blind to connection.
Stories disconnected to the whole.

Tension filled the air.
A great tension fell upon the people.
It filled them.
Dread was everywhere.

The woman...she was quiet.
She did not speak.

Children began to run everywhere!
They did run.
And shout.
Some danced.
Laughter filled the skies.

Rules disappeared.

The woman...she was quiet.
She did not speak.

The children...they did feel it...

A formless birth.
Invisible.
They saw what could not be seen.

They celebrated.
The children...they did celebrate.

Tension fled.
Nowhere to hide.

The woman...she was quiet.
She did not speak.

April 11, 2015, 5:20–6:10 p.m.
Lake Shastina, California

As I sat in the silence...these words did come...the signs were everywhere.
I knew that a new parable was arriving about the birthed world of love.

She Saw the Illusion

She saw the illusion.
She saw it many times.
Glimpses came. Big ones. Small ones.

She never knew when she would clearly see.
Often it came unbidden.
Often it came and went as the wind.
Appearing for a moment.
And gone.
As a lover come to play.

At twelve years, the seeing opened…
For an instant she stood six feet tall…
alone and seeing…
Seeing from the back of the head…
And it closed…
She told no one…

On a boat to Crete came a dream…

an infant…awake in this dream…
an infant…in Christed knowing…

And came a collision for a second…
in the Timeless…it seemed Infinity…
In the Timeless…a love with no opposite presides…
and joy…endless joy…
and life in this dream does change…

The openings…they increased.
Coming often as whispers on the wind…
And silence…
And stillness that has no end….

The openings…as gifts cast from heaven…
The openings…unfettered world of unworldly love…
Luring…
Seducing…
Calling from beyond the good, the bad…

Ever the unseen lover…
Undressing the physical form…

Ever the unseen Lover…
Unveiling the world of form…
Ever the illusion…exposed…
Naked even…

Even…it is…orgasms exposed…
a portal…not a destination…
and the door closes.

Again and again…the door closes…
needing it again…and again…
Thirsting for it…as water…
Never is it enough…

Lost…is the knowing…that IT never leaves…
IT does not come and go…

And portals…there are none…
From this realm…portals never were…

Awareness looks about…
the seer never leaves…

Doubts and beliefs...borne of fear...
They do cast some shadows...for a bit...
Creating make-believe and let's pretend...

Awareness looks about...
And the seer never leaves...

People...they build cities...nations...
They do rise and fall...

Awareness looks about...
The seer never leaves...

People...they build empires...kill and loot...
And empires crumble and turn to dust...

Awareness looks about...
The seer never leaves...

Light has always ruled...
It has always reigned...
All are always seers...

Awareness looks about...
The seer never leaves...

Tribes do form...
Everywhere...tribes do form...
They dance...
They dance beyond illusion...
They dance beyond the time...

From the formless...the Tribes do form...
Everywhere...the tribes do form...
And everywhere...Infinity begins to dance...

Awareness looks about...
The seer never leaves...

April 16, 2015, 8:55 a.m.
Lake Shastina, California

This morning of my birthday, the subject of illusions and this illusory dimension continued to pour into my thoughts.

So I sat empty, watching thoughts come and go until the words, "she saw the illusion" did come. They felt different. I wrote them down and the universal story birthed.

And just before the story came, I continued to be aware of how unimportant our concepts about birthday age are, yet how much wisdom awaits inside of us. And if we are vigilant, we shall be aware of that waiting wisdom.

The elders, that have focussed on the Inner Presence, have not only a perspective that is an aerial view, but they also begin to see how it fits together.

From this singularity, the kaleidoscopic forms of life are ever more beautiful mandalas of life. From the seeming sense of separation from that singularity are created distortions and even perversions of the ever perfect mandala. This perfection is ever to be experienced and loved!

Her

She saw the sun.
She saw the sky.
She saw the river flowing by.

She sees the path
That people take.
And all the love
Some people fake.

She saw the sun.
She saw the moon.
She saw that everything was in tune.

She sees the birds
Flying high.
She sees the bees
Buzzing by.

She heard the roaring of the wind.

Then came her angel.
There she stood.

She felt so good.
She could fly.
She really couldn't ever die.

She sees the whispers
Coming by
Soaring quickly to the sky.

They spiraled up.
They spiraled down.
They spiraled quickly
To the ground.

I can feel.
I can hear.
I can see.
I can be.

And with that she understood.

Love cannot be unhooked.

She only saw
And never spoke.
All her love
Came with hope.

She flew up high
To the sky.
All her love
Pouring by.

She made an impact
On the world.
There she stands;
Her voice is heard.

So if you hear her voice again
Listen close to find true love again.

You never know
What you can miss

Without a hug or a kiss.

You never know what you can find
Like an angel soaring high.

By Maya Rose Rawitch, 12 years of age
April, 2015

Maya says she was inspired after hearing a reading of She Sees the Illusion.

Maya says that the poem came to her quickly. She wrote. She became aware of the words as they dropped into consciousness.

Ecstatic Writing

In this book of parables and in all the forms that inspire me, I have simply been quiet, empty, open. I have pen and paper. I am surrendered. An immense feeling of simplicity comes upon me. Much like an empty canvas. And begins...ecstatic writing.

As the new earth culture continues to birth, more and more people shall exalt in this sacred allowing of form after form to emerge.

Giving birth to love. Being and doing as one.

The poetic and mystical parables allow one to reflect on one's own life and allow ever deeper awareness to arise as pure consciousness.

The parables have been used by ones to initiate creativity, writing and insight. They exist as "poetic muses" exuding essence of life.

They are best read quietly and slowly by oneself. Even out loud. Or one may have another read slowly to you. Close your eyes and "see," feel and experience the story. Allow it to commune with you. It is best to remain in stillness for a time after the reading.

The Experience of Ecstatic Writing

My experience with Ecstatic Writing is that it comes usually unbidden. It comes when it comes.

As a lover in the night or at dawn. And sometimes... anytime. The receiver of the words, spaces, tones, enchantment must be a yin lover, ever alert, present and receptive. With no thoughts. Empty.

The writings come as almost incantations to elevate the mind. An alchemy is felt as a most sublime essence. Beauty landing. Formless in form.

It is a sacred act. Exaltation comes.

As the transcendent energy mysteriously forms as words in Consciousness, it has its own life. It has its own intonations, rhythms and cadence. And even space.

I simply pass them on choosing font, format, spaces and art that enhance the essence and existence of the writing. The art of book design, done by conscious book designers, creates the sacred environment for the story to land in this dimension. Softly...inviting...

In my books, everything is chosen to best convey the transcendent meaning and message in the story. This allows a deeper soul reading.

Below is a description of how space, font, format have been used as an art form.

They are the temple garments for the ceremonial space for grace to land.

1. Extra space between the lines allows one's soul to more easily read, see and feel beyond the lines. Soul reading.

2. Larger margins give the added feeling of space to feel into the spaciousness of the Vastness.

3. A scripted font invokes a poetic response.

4. All of these things allow for a slower and deeper reading, that a deeper communing with the stories may happen.

In the process of landing the story into a book, one clearly sees the importance of the art of book design. For it is part of the meaning and message, as well as housing the language of the soul. It is as a temple space.

The art form of the book is integral to the birth. It is not done for commercial reasons. It is integral to the soul of the book in its wholeness. Container and contained. One. An emergence. Spirit AS matter. One.

Attunement Guidelines
for Parables

The parables may be read by individuals and/or used for group meditation, contemplation and sharing.

Meditative Reading

Read and/or listen to the parable while you are empty. Be open and receptive.

No need to understand with the mind. No need to analyze or debate or opinionate.

The parables are best read slowly with a rhythm and cadence that is like the shape of the writing. Notice and feel the space between the lines and in the margins. That is space for the soul to feel deeply its response. It creates space for insight and direct knowing.

In the Emptiness of Being, one will quite naturally understand the story in one's own unique and distinct way. There is no right or wrong way. One may begin to feel embodied presence.

Contemplation

1. Allow yourself to see how the parable/story relates to your own life and awakening.

2. Allow yourself to envision how the parable/story relates to the global shift of consciousness.

   See this consciousness-shift free of the human sense of right and wrong, good and evil. See this shift as the arising Impersonal Consciousness. From a sense of personal I to the Impersonal I. From a sense of human self to Soul Self. This is noticing from a more expanded awareness.

3. Allow yourself to perceive ever greater glimpses, insights, visions and revelations of the new earth culture that is emerging.

4. Allow yourself to realize your beautiful and perfect soul expression in the new earth culture that is upon us all.

5. How might these parables herald an expanded vision of the new and precious consciousness that is birthing?

6. What is the deepest meaning/purpose that you can find for the parables?

7. How may this universal story catalyze, inspire and initiate deep meaning and experience in your individual life? How may it further ignite the collective soul?

8. Do you see anyone else's life that the parable might inspire?

9. What stands out in the parable/story? Why? How is it relevant to your life and the collective life?

10. How are these parables universal?

11. How are these parables in service to seeing beyond the belief in the sense of separation from the Infinite?

12. Find the denouement of one of the parables, that speaks most strongly to you. This dramatic turning point is the same one that humanity is in as it moves from a sense of individual consciousness to elevated Consciousness.

Contemplation for Specific Parables

Below are some ideas to contemplate from specific parables. You may begin to ask and share your own questions for other parables.

The Watcher: A Girl from the Stars

1. Everyone is a watcher. Speak of yourself as a watcher. Do you trust yourself? Do you act on what you see? Do you act on

what you know? Do you act on your living revelations?

The Worshippers: And the Sound of Star Light And this One from the Stars

1. Where is the moment in this soul story where "the one" becomes The One? And how do you feel about that?

2. Where are you on this journey of "getting" or "giving" as a way of being? Do you see the universal law of supply?

3. Scan the planet in your consciousness and look at all the watchers, beholders, witnesses, observers and monitors.

4. Notice the many ways "watchers" serve. Examples are documentaries and films that expose the old and ones that reveal the new. Also there are national and international organizations that are monitoring our environment. What others examples can you see?

1. Describe what you felt as you read or heard this story. Be aware of the importance of deep feeling as a soul faculty.

2. How does this relate to music you have heard?

3. Does this story sound far-fetched or does it catalyze other experiences you have had? What are they?

4. What are some real life activities that are occurring world wide, where you see this happening with groups?

The Oracle and the Dreamer

1. What does it mean for the dream to enter the field?

2. Who or what is the oracle in our own world?

3. What is the value in purity to the awakening collective?

she sings to the earth

1. Does talking about the meaning add or detract from your essence experience, the soul-felt sense of the parable?

2. What is the Unspeakable? The Unutterable? How may that come into your life more fully?

3. How may your "song to the earth" be expressed more fully? And do you have one?

and still...she came...

1. How does "The Great Time," that is The Timeless Realm, affect your world? The collective's world?

O we all are oracles

1. How do the veils fall via joy?

2. Why is the collective so obsessed and burdened with the belief in fear?

3. How may you free yourself of this collective belief in fear and its offsprings?

This Village

1. Is the consciousness world in which the old man lives...practical? How?

The Signs Were Everywhere

1. What signs of the new culture do you see?

2. How does one see the "heaven's script?"

She Saw the Illusion

1. What does "love with no opposites" mean?

2. What does it mean that "It does not come and go?"

3. What does it mean that "the seer never leaves?"

4. What does it mean to "dance beyond illusion?"

About the Artist, Writer, Spiritual Educator

Mystic artist, spiritual educator, writer, Mary Saint-Marie, expresses formless Essence of the One in many different forms. Painting, sculpture, poetry, poetic odysseys, passages, parables, multi-media presentations, sounds and signings of the soul and a play.

Mary also "holds sacred space" for ones individually as Soul Sessions and in groups via workshops and retreats. This allows people to experience their Spiritual Identity and begin to drop the beliefs that seem to separate us from the One Self.

Mary grew to love a powerful freedom through extraordinary time in nature as a child. This was her spiritual teacher. She had no words for this unfettered sense of joy and freedom. She could feel the peace, the inner joy. That became the guiding Light of Being. Nature was the friend. Ever present.

For a number of years, soul choices were laid aside to do society's world, until a near death experience awoke her to a greatly expanded awareness of joy, love, freedom, outside of the human mind's ability to know. The Realm of Soul.

The near death experience birthed a fully new awareness and life. For now Mary had deeply felt the field of light that is ever present. Once this state of exalted awareness is experienced, there is no turning back.

Even if only a glimpse, this soul realm exudes love that has no opposite. It is the "It" that the world searches for, longs for.

The new life

The artistic creations began to flow into manifestation as continual revelations borne of the realms of light. Journeys to many soul realms/dimensions continued to come. Some spontaneously. Some via meditation. Some in lucid dreams.

After leaving college English teaching, Mary left on an extended journey across the Middle East, India, Kashmir, Crete, Morocco, etc. Mary Saint-Marie began pioneering visionary art shows in 1972. Her Art-of-the-Soul has been viewed in more than 150 exhibits, in galleries, expositions, faires, workshops and conferences. Mary's sacred art is in private collections around the nation and the world. The visionary art has been featured on TV interviews, cards, calendars, cds and on and in magazines and books. Most recently the art was featured in the documentary, FEMME:Women Healing the World.

Mary was a sacred enactment performance artist for seven years, with her multi-media enactment, She...it is...who Remembers. It included her narration, art, soul sounding, dancing and music by exceptional musicians.

Mary also wrote and produced a play that she wrote via a dream and the state between waking and dreaming. The Monitor and Laughter of the Gods: Saraswati Comes Swingin' Her Hips is the story of universal balance of the masculine and feminine principle. It is sacred theatre reflecting Awareness of our Oneness.

Mary lives in the mountains and high desert of Northern California.

Art, Books, Sessions, and Retreats

Art

Fine Art Giclee Reproductions are available.
Inquire about original art.

Books

Books may be ordered on Amazon.

Galactic Shamanism
The Sacred Two
The Holy Sight
Nectar of Woman
Messages from the Silence
The Star-Stone Two
The Animating Presence
The Monitor and Laughter of the Gods
Art as Consciousness

CDs

Soul Sounds of World Birth
Journey of Consciousness

Website gives more information about Mystic Art, Soul Sessions, Soul Retreats and Holy Sight workshops.

Note the youtube videos and interviews.

www.marysaintmarie.com

www.EarthCareGlobalTV.com

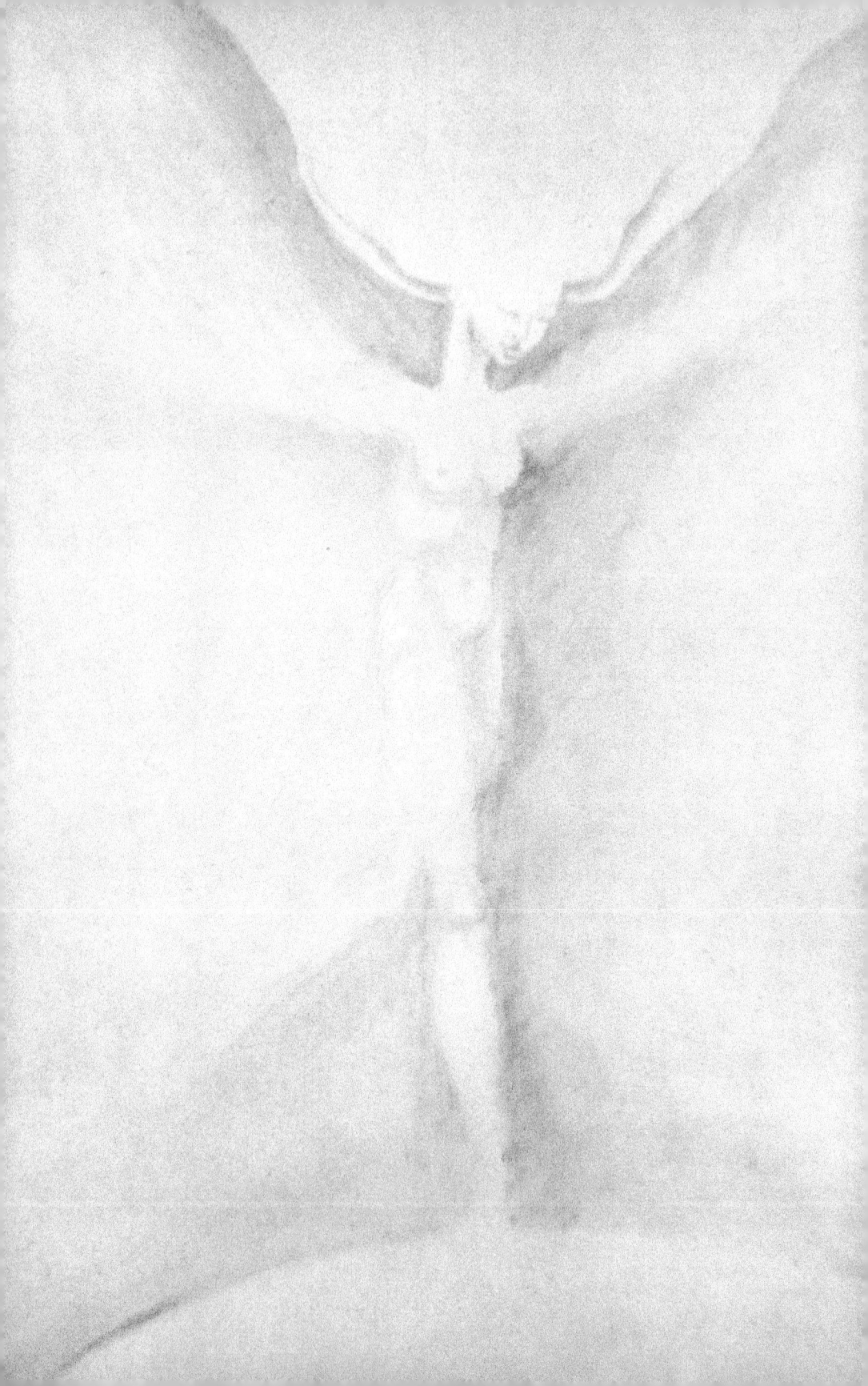

Being the emptiness that we already are
allows the flow of the Infinite to play
through us and as us.

We are the sacred vessel through which
the creative intelligence flows.
We ever allow divine inspirations to come.
We ever allow Vision to land.

In this way, we are the lover and Beloved as One.
We are that sacred synapse point
where sense of separation dissolves.

The formless…as form…
The Invisible…visible…
The Unspeakable with voice…

www.ingramcontent.com/pod-product-compliance
Lightning Source LLC
Chambersburg PA
CBHW050411030726
47503CB00006B/2143